Eunice and Kate

by Mariana Llanos  illustrated by Elena Napoli

penny candy BOOKS

Penny Candy Books
Oklahoma City & Greensboro

Text © 2020 Mariana Llanos
Illustrations © 2020 Elena Napoli

Photo of Mariana Llanos: Carlos Ortiz
Design: Shanna Compton

24 23 22 21 20   1 2 3 4 5
ISBN-13: 978-0-9996584-7-5 (hardcover)

Small press. Big conversations.
www.pennycandybooks.com

*To my mom, for guiding my dreams
with patience and wisdom. —ML*

Eunice and Kate lived in side-by-side apartments in the heart of the city.

They shared the same playground in winter and the same pool in summer.

Their mothers did laundry in the same basement room with its flaky, musty walls. Eunice and Kate helped fold clothes.

Their mothers shared stories, while
Eunice and Kate shared their dreams.

Eunice's mama worked at the bakery.
Sometimes, she sank her head in her
hands and said she couldn't afford things.

But Mama had endless laughter, like the waves of the sea. Her kisses were as sweet as the pastries she decorated.

Kate's mom worked at the hair salon.
Sometimes, she blushed when she had to
count her last coins to pay for Kate's clothes.

But Mom's laugh was bright
like the stars, and her kisses
were as smooth as the cream
she used on people's hair.

Eunice dreamed of being a ballet dancer. She twirled and leaped clumsily, but one day she would be as graceful as a crane.

Kate dreamed of being an astronaut. She soared to the stars in a homemade spaceship, but one day she would lead a mission to Mars.

Eunice and Kate went to school together every day. Eunice pirouetted like a dancer on stage. Kate hopped giant lunar steps.

In their classroom they shared glue, scissors, and a box of crayons.

One day, when it was time to draw a portrait of each other, they opened their eyes and observed.

Eunice wasn't sure being an astronaut would be any fun for Kate, so she drew her friend as a lovely ballet dancer instead.

Kate didn't think dancing ballet
was adventurous enough for
Eunice, so she drew her friend
as a mighty space traveler.

Eunice and Kate looked at
each other's drawings.

"That's not me," said Kate.

"That's not me, either!" said Eunice.

Could a ballet dancer and an astronaut be friends anyway?

They walked home separately for the first time ever. Each girl showed her mom what the other had done.

Kate's mom said, "I love
the laughter she drew on your
face. She knows you well."

Eunice's mom said, "Look at the lovely color she used for your big heart. She knows you well."

Eunice stared at her portrait
for a long time. Kate stared
out the window.

Then, almost at the same time,
they grabbed their crayons
and began to work.

"I thought you might like to dance on the moon," Kate said, as she handed Eunice her new portrait the next morning.

"And maybe we could defy gravity onstage someday!" said Eunice.

Eunice and Kate walked together to school like always. And when it started to rain, they shared an umbrella.

Mariana Llanos is a Peruvian-born writer of children's literature. She has published several children's books, including the bilingual *Luca's Bridge/El puente de Luca* (Penny Candy Books, 2019) and the award-winning bilingual books *Kutu: The Tiny Inca Princess* (Campoy-Ada Awards), *Poesia Alada* (International Latino Book Awards), and *Tristan Wolf* (IPNE Book Awards), among others. In 2017, Mariana received the Oklahoma Human Rights Award for her work visiting schools around the world via virtual technology, to promote literacy. That same year she was selected as the Best Latino Artist by the Hispanic Arts Council of Oklahoma. Mariana developed an early love for reading and writing in her native Peru. She studied theater in Lima then moved to the United States where she decided to pursue her passion: to become a children's author. She dedicates her time to creating multicultural, poignant, and engaging stories and lives with her husband and their three children in Oklahoma City, Oklahoma.

Elena Napoli is an Italian illustrator and character designer who studied entertainment design at the NEMO Academy of Digital Arts in Florence. Growing up in the Italian art scene, she has drawn for as long as she can remember and has always known that making art would be her future. Starting with digital and traditional techniques, like watercolor and ecoline, Elena initially focused on animated films and then moved to illustrations. Among her interests are music, young adult fiction, children's books, indie video games, films and TV series, as well as her dream of traveling doing what she loves and finding her own place in the world. She lives in Bristol, UK.